A Web of Tragedy

(Book of short stories part1)

BY

CHERYL. T. LONG

(A COLLECTION OF FOUR NOVELLAS)

Table of Contents

A FAIR DEAL

Chapter 1

NOT THAT HE WAS EXACTLY AFRAID OF DEATH. He was after all the only local mortician in Chessington. There was definitely not another – from the overpopulated town of Lincoln, Nebraska, to the very reach of Harper's Groove, which was in downtown Chessington. No, Kenneth Long wasn't really afraid of death. He had seen more than his fair share of it, to be riled thus.

Now, it must be clearly noted that even though Kenneth was no longer unnerved or afraid of death, due to the simple fact that he had seen too many a death as his position as town's mortician and undertaker entailed, he was quite wary of the thought of dying. The act of dying, not death, was the dark cloud in Gary Norman's sky. It was the red balloon floating amidst a conspicuous pool of black balloons. Ever so present at the back of his aging mind.

Only the day before, after the bell for the evening mass tolled at the local church down by Carpenter Lane, another body had been brought in. Kenneth took one look at the body and could almost tell the cause of the death, by just glancing at it.

It was the body of Tina Bernard, the wife of Byron Bernard, and from the way her skin seemed dried and congealed, and the way her lips drew back tightly against her teeth, almost in a snarl, Kenneth was sure Tina had died of consumption.

He had taken the liberty of placing her body on the steel table in his backroom, which also served an autopsy room. Byron Bernard, who was still in deep mourning, had made a great sorrowful fuss about wanting to see the remains of his wife once more, before interment. Of course, this was a request that Kenneth didn't grant. He merely dismissed it as the ramblings of a grieving man. There was actually little time to accommodate such petty sentiments. Her body needed to be disposed of as soon as possible.

There she was, on the steel table, which was illuminated by the beam of the single halogen bulb. She was naked, with a small name tag that Kenneth had attached to the toe on her right leg. This tag was the only means of identifying some of the bodies that were being preserved in the town's morgue. Most times, these bodies get disfigured, distorted, and unrecognizable due to rot. There were bodies that still lay in the lockers, unclaimed by anyone, be it family, friend, or relative. Such bodies were eventually sent to the crematorium to be cremated.

Her bones were pinched tight against the whitening skin, her eyes, which were closed, appeared to be sunken in, most of her hair had fallen off – still one of the virulent symptoms of the disease, which had finally laid claim to her life. Her cheekbones were quite visible, and as Kenneth opened her mouth, he was not too startled by what he saw – a blackened and swollen tongue.

Nodding his head in affirmation, he took down notes. His grey eyes stole glimpses at the corpse, which was still on his table as he scribbled away on his paper:

NAME: TINA ROSALEE LONG

GENDER: FEMALE

DESCRIPTION; WHITE FEMALE, IN HER LATE 30'S

CAUSE OF DEATH: CONSUMPTION.

RECOMMENDED METHOD OF INTERMENT: CREMATION

It was quite glaring; the disease had caused her to waste away. It had been progressive, continuous, and Kenneth could also imagine how painful it'd have been for her. The very thought only made him shudder.

He could almost imagine how the illness worked its way through her vital organs, turning them inside out, causing her untold pains before finally killing her off.

Kenneth sighed heavily and wheeled her body back in the locker; he made a mental note of having the body cremated by evening. All that remained now was to have a little chat with Holt, who was still in the waiting room in the morgue alongside a friend.

Locking the door behind him, he strode down the hallway, which was quite dark. As he approached the main hall, he could make out the men seated at the far corner. The other man was Jim Faulkner, and he had a hand on Bryon, patting the sobbing man.

Kenneth announced his presence with a cough, and both men looked up at him. Bryon scrambled up hastily and rushed at him frantically.

"Tell me we're going to give her a decent burial," he sobbed, holding onto Kenneth's lapel. "She deserves better than all of this."

Kenneth placed his hands gently on the older man. "Look, Bryon, I understand how you feel. But you know the county rules ever since the plague started — no burials for victims of consumption. The best way to limit its spread is by cremation," he said, abruptly removing the leather gloves from his hands and disposing them off in a refuse can.

"You can't do that to her!" Bryon cried. "She deserves better." This time, the sob racked through his body as he buried his face in Kenneth's chest and cried harder.

"C'mon Bryon; you just have to man up to this." Jim chipped in, patting Bryon on the back. "Trust me, she sure won't like you tearing up like this; she would have wanted you to be strong."

"Yeah, Bryon, you've got to take heart; I know how hard this is." Kenneth added, still comforting the sobbing man.

"I guess so," Bryon muttered, his body quivering with each word. "I promised her a new sewing kit. It actually arrived today. She'll never get to use it, and I'll never hear her happy songs again by the porch as she works on my socks."

This was Bryon's last statement as he allowed himself to be led down to the crematorium by Kenneth and Jim. There was no more crying or sobbing, as the bereaved husband looked upon the face of his once beautiful wife for the last time, a face that had wasted away from consumption. After this, Kenneth proceeded to cremate the body, and all the men watched it burn.

About an hour later, the morgue was once more empty. Kenneth had sat by his table in his office and smoked his pipe, the event of that evening – if you could really call it an event, had been just a daily ritual for him. It was after all his duty to take care of the dead and comfort the living, something that he had done satisfactorily.

Blowing wisps of smoke into the air and watching it float and disperse, merging with the blankness of the office, his mind sort of relaxed. Perhaps, he would make a stop at Great London's Pizza and grab a slice or so. He was as hungry as a starving wolf. There was also the fact that he had to make a call to Doctor Pecker, the town's physician, who had requested his immediate attention as regards an issue.

Kenneth and Doctor Pecker never really got along, and that was because the latter always found fault in his work as the mortician, and Kenneth knew he did the work pretty well. Well, there was really no choice in the matter. He would make the call to see him and try not to lose his cool.

Thinking about these things, Kenneth drifted off.

A gentle breeze caressed his skin, and something brushed past his neck. Kenneth started up almost immediately. He peered around hazily. His office had grown considerably dark; there was no telling how long he had slept.

He stood up and groped around the office, looking for the switch. His fingers snaked through the wall and flicked on the switch, which would have provided light through a single bulb in the room.

No light came on.

Damned power supply, Kenneth thought bitterly, thrusting his hand into his pocket, he fished out a flashlight.

A thin ray of light swept across the room as he turned it on. His fingers wrapped around the handle of the door and pulled it open. The wind flared up his brown hair as he stepped into the hallway.

Someone sniggered lightly behind him, and Kenneth whirled around; his heart thudding in his chest.

"Who's there?" he called loudly. But only silence replied. "If anyone's out there, trying to play a stupid joke, just quit right now and leave me to lock up. It's way past my bedtime as it is"

Not a single sound came back.

Kenneth stared ahead into the emptiness of the hallway, which led directly to the autopsy room. And that was when he saw her - the woman that he had cremated that evening, staring right back at him.

Chapter 2

He blinked twice. It was only the shadow of the file cabinet at the far end of the hallway. For a moment, he could have sworn that his heart had almost jumped into his mouth. His arms were soon covered in gooseflesh as he made his way out of the morgue.

Putting on his coat, he tried as much as possible to remove the face of Tina Bernard from his mind. And as he stepped out into the serene night – he was able to do just that.

The walk down to Great London's wasn't very hectic. Kenneth, who was still quite agile for a man in his late forties, strode briskly along the curb-side, sometimes waving back when he was greeted by someone or smiling unevenly when he was accosted by one of the locals who was fortunate enough to recognize him.

A signpost was soon in view, and even though it was almost way past midnight, there were about six people all waiting in line for a slice of pizza and perhaps, a Diet Coke.

Kenneth joined the line and waited. Sometimes, he would hum a familiar tune, screeching under his breath. After he had been attended to, he paid and would have gone on his way when someone touched his arm.

He turned around almost sharply, to find Doctor Pecker smiling at him. Kenneth frowned; he had not expected to see the old doctor until the following evening.

"Howdy Kenneth, never thought I'd see you here." Doctor Pecker chuckled, patting Kenneth on the back.

"I'd say the same for you, Doc. So, what brings you out to Great London's? Not the pizza, I hope," Kenneth asked.

"Partly; yes, and no, basically, this is actually about you."

"About me?"

Doctor Pecker only nodded his head slowly in affirmation. There was an aura of gloom in the way that the doctor had said those words.

"I did everything as you asked, not a single body is left at the crematorium. I still had one cremated tonight, but you must try to see reason, Doc. Some of these people insist on wanting to have –" Kenneth started.

Doctor Pecker only raised one hand and cut short Kenneth's ramblings. "It isn't about any of those things, Kenneth, it's about you. Remember the routine medical check that I asked you to go for?"

Kenneth nodded his head, "Certainly, so what's wrong?"

"Well, I had to run more tests to confirm this. I couldn't afford to keep it from you, knowing that you would one day eventually get to know," Doctor Pecker said.

Those eyes remained fixated on the Doctor. "Tell me what you got."

"We just discovered that you may have cancer. I know this is probably not the right place and time to be discussing it. Ensure you come by my office, Kenneth; this is no joke." Doctor Pecker blurted out hastily.

The words that flew out of the mouth of the doctor were long replaced by incoherent gibberish, which ushered Kenneth Long into a world hidden from sight.

For the first time, Kenneth Long thought about dying. If what Doctor Pecker was saying is the truth, he knew he had little time to live. There was no cure for his illness, and this he knew quite well. Like a man caught in a gypsy's trance, Kenneth wandered off from the doctor and went to the other side of the road and threw up. Well, it was happening sooner than he could ever think. Feeling full of despair Kenneth eyes shot straight up to the sky as to be pleading to the forces of the beyond. He soon scanned the area and spotted Hubert's bar.

Chapter 3

The taste of the whiskey he had ordered from Hubert had some kind of metallic taste. Kenneth sipped the drink again, the metallic taste intensified, and he gagged – almost retching.

"You okay, sir?" came the voice of the bartender, the bar was mostly empty, save a few people who were scattered around the tables, scantily; playing cards, chattering away excitedly like boisterous school kids and making out with some women.

Filtering softly from the music box was *Gloomy Sunday* by Theodore Sect, a song that brought a kind of tranquil-like atmosphere to the bar.

Kenneth downed another shot of whiskey, which burned his throat and almost made him retch again. But this was something that he managed to control.

"You okay, Mr. Long?" Hubert, the bartender, repeated, looking quite concerned.

"Yes, never mind about me, Hubert. I think I'm gonna be just fine." Kenneth replied sullenly. He ordered another drink, which the bartender refilled for him.

There was no doubt about it. Pecker had ruined his evening, his work, and finally his life. It was almost hard to believe that he would be dying soon; it sounded absurd.

Kenneth had a few more drinks and left the bar in a haze. He stumbled all the way home feeling like someone was following behind him. Kenneth woke up the next morning with a hang over but still remember what Doctor Pecker told him the night before. Kenneth pictured his death all day. He pictured being sick and being cremated. Kenneth cried and worried all night. The next morning he decided to go see Doctor Pecker.

Chapter 4

"So, how much time do you reckon that I have left?" he had asked Doctor Pecker after he had thrown up his lunch earlier.

"About eight months, or nine months, if you're lucky. But there's no need to be too hard on yourself; there has been some advancement in medical science that I hope will certainly take care of this situation of yours." Doctor Pecker said with a note of confidence.

"What advancement? I thought there was no cure," Kenneth asked, at the back of his already panicking mind, there was a faint ray of hope.

"It's called Chemotherapy. This would help slow down the growth of the cancerous cells and help reduce your chances of dying. However, it's an expensive treatment and –"

"How much?"

"It's not only about that Kenneth, there are also some side effects which are worth mentioning," Doctor Pecker added.

"What side effects? If this thing that you have mentioned can cure me, I see no reason why I can't endure one or two side effects," Kenneth insisted. There was some sort of desperation in his voice, even though his work so far as a local mortician allowed him only the meagre income of seventy dollars per month, he had taken time to save more than enough of it. This – he was ready to spend if it was going to aid the furthering of the treatment.

"Most patients who undergo chemo," Doctor Pecker explained. "Often end up losing most of their hair due to the violent exposure to radiation. There are other side effects, but this gets better with time."

Kenneth sighed. "Tell me where do I have to go for treatment? So, I can start the treatment for immediately."

"That's great. Just go home Kenneth, we'll get you set up as soon as possible." I'll walk with you outside as I need to go see Mrs. Walker at the nursing home. Doctor Pecker had patted his shoulder before getting into his Sedan and driving down the dusty road of Pillsbury Way, leaving Kenneth to gawk after him, watching the trail of dust disappear into the air.

There was no going home for him. He had found himself in the bar again somehow and had proceeded to start drinking once more. In a way, this helped him forget his troubles. It was just ironic. Not even the treatment being offered could really set his mind at ease, he was afraid.

Still pondering about all these things, he didn't see the man – dressed in a black cloak with a hood, settle down beside him. He didn't see that the eyes of this man were unusual and quite menacing. He definitely didn't see the odd wiry smile on the face of this man.

Kenneth didn't see these things because he was already quite drunk. Most of his senses numb, and the room only seemed to spin around, as he staggered away from the bar stand. His legs wobbled under him and would have given way if the man who had been watching him had not caught him by the waist and steadied him on his feet.

"Hello, Kenneth." The man in the dark cloak cooed.

Chapter 5

Kenneth gaped at the man in surprise. He must have been, at least, a foot taller than him, and there was this charisma or aura around the man that made Kenneth want to respect him.

"How did you know mmy nammme?" Kenneth stuttered, very astonished.

The man in the dark cloak only responded by taking off his hood. He was definitely one of the finest men that Kenneth had ever seen. His eyes were sky blue, and his nose and mouth were perfectly set like a carved out bust. There was no visible expression on his face; it was like looking at a blank piece of paper.

"Does that really matter, Kenneth?" he finally responded. "Why I'm here is much more consequential than how I got to know your name," the man said. Waving his right hand at Hubert, the man called for a shot of Wild Turkey whiskey, which was brought to him consequently.

Kenneth only looked on in silence as the man downed the drink without flinching. There was also something about the way he talked that made Kenneth wonder if he was even from Chessington. He was certainly not one of the locals – Kenneth knew almost everyone in the town.

"You're thinking about how possible it is that you don't recognize me. You don't have to; I'm not from around here," the man said.

Kenneth gasped.

Perhaps, he had hallucinated it, but that didn't seem to be the case. Did this man just tell him his thoughts?

The man in the dark cloak smiled. "Don't be startled or afraid, and this is not a hallucination. I came to talk to you and perhaps to help you with your recent problem."

"Problem?" Kenneth said, almost reflectively. "I don't know what you're talking about, sire."

"Of course, you do. Didn't your doctor just assure you that you got a huge guillotine in the form of a cancer hanging over your neck?" the man in the cloak asked.

Kenneth jerked up from his table and cringed back from the man in terror.

"Sit down, Kenneth." The man in the cloak instructed emphatically.

Still looking dazed, Kenneth obeyed the instruction and sat down on the barstool again, how could he have known that? He had barely known until about two hours ago following the bad news from Doctor Pecker.

"No need contemplating how I knew, I can see the disease inside of you, Kenneth, and it won't stop until you're dead. Forget about that so-called treatment, that won't do much either. You don't want to die now, do you?" the man in the cloak asked.

Kenneth shook his head frantically, for the first time in a really long while, since the death of his mother, he allowed his tears flow freely.

"For a man that has seen all kinds of death, you sure suck at keeping it together," the man in the cloak commented.

"I don't want to die!" Kenneth moaned, "I'm scared of the whole process; it has always been my worst fear."

The man in the cloak chuckled at that. "Pretty much, no one wants to die, Kenneth. Trust me, death does suck. Tina Bernard can testify."

This comment didn't unnerve Kenneth. If the man could know all about his health and job, why wouldn't he know about the woman whom Kenneth had cremated only the night before?

"But for a mortician, you shouldn't be afraid of death. It is just like going to sleep. Nothing really special about sleeping – the only difference is; you don't get to wake up anymore," the man in the dark cloak said.

"But I still don't want to die. How do you know so much about me?" Kenneth asked.

"Oh, I don't really know anything, Kenneth. I can only know the things that you allow me to know. Well, you're pretty much depressed about your health. That's how I got to know about the cancer."

"Can anything be done? Anything at all? If this chemo doesn't work, is there no other way for me?"

The man in the cloak tapped on the table as if in deep thought, considering the questions that Kenneth had asked. Then after a minute of silence or two had passed, he proceeded to say, "Well, I have made a few deals with people like you in the past, I'm a businessman, Kenneth. I love doing business, but the question is, are you ready to do business with me?"

"Yes, but what kind of business? And how does that relate to helping my unhealthy condition?" Kenneth asked.

"Relax, Kenneth. As I said, I'm a man of business. Lots of men have been in your position Kenneth, and I have been able to strike them a deal here or there. Once, I helped a talented blind artist regain his sight and he, in turn, offered me his soul. But I didn't need his soul anyway; all I wanted was a nice painting of myself. At yet another time, I helped another man who had a money problem in exchange for a sacrifice of one of his virgin daughters – I happen to have a thing or two for virgin blood. So, I love making fair deals, Kenneth I can offer you a deal, but what do you have to offer me in return?"

Kenneth gaped at the man. "You're actually joking about everything you just said, right?"

The man in the cloak laughed heartily. "I never knew I was humorous. That's funny, Kenneth, but I wasn't joking. I wish I had the wit to make jokes, but I have been too serious for all of eternity."

"But how can that be possible? You don't look old."

"Quite long-lived, yes. But that's not the case here, Kenneth. Do you want to do business or not?"

"Assuming I decided to do business with you, do I get to tell you what I want most? And what's the assurance that you can get it done?" Kenneth furthered.

"That would basically depend on what you have to offer me, and it has to be something worth what you're asking for, anything short of that, and the deal's off," the man in the cloak replied. "Tell me what you want most, Kenneth, what you crave for most?"

"Immortality," he blurted out without thinking. "I don't want to ever age, and I don't want to die, I want to just live forever".

"Interesting deal. Well, I can arrange that for you, but what do I get in return, Kenneth? Like I said, you have to offer me something worth what you're asking for."

"My soul?" Kenneth said, almost tentatively.

"What makes you think that your soul would be worth anything to me? Most souls are already damned anyway, so there's actually no need to collect them if they'll still come to you," the man in the cloak pointed out.

"I don't know what else to offer you. I don't think you'll collect money or anything of that sort – if not, I would have offered you over ten thousand dollars that I have saved up; mostly in bonds and shares, which I was looking forward to using in the last days of my life," Kenneth said.

The man in the cloak nodded his head in understanding. "Okay, I understand your plight and would help you. Are you ready to offer me your services? Pledge your loyalty to me and help me collect some really pure souls in exchange for what you have asked me for?"

"I will do anything, but how would my services be useful to you? I'm only a mortician. All I know is about death, and here I'm trying to avoid it. What good would my services bring to you?"

"Worry yourself not about such matters, Kenneth, just pledge to me, and I'll find a way to grant you your wish." The man in the cloak said.

"Okay, I'm ready. What do I need to do?"

"Good, all you have to do is; sign this paper." the man in cloak procured a pen, which didn't really look like any pen that Kenneth had ever seen in his entire life and a small parchment which had some words scribbled on it faintly.

Kenneth took the pen from the man in the cloak, and as he held onto it, he could see that the empty ink-line was filling up with something red, bright pain flared through his right hand.

"Don't drop the pen, Kenneth, just endure the pain and sign. That pen of mine has struck many a fair deal in the past. Did I mention that I once struck a deal with Paganini? Ever heard of him? A great violinist – he wrote me some great music, which I still listen to. That one was indeed talented."

Kenneth didn't hear these things as he struggled to sign the parchment. After he was done, the pain receded, and he handed over the paper to the man in the cloak. "Is that all I need to do?"

"Of course, that would be all, Kenneth; I will be here in about a year from now. Just to see how things are coming along, then we can start our work." The man in the cloak replied.

"That's assuming I'm not dead and gone before you are back." Kenneth chuckled at that.

"Trust me, you won't be," the man said, rising to his feet and shaking hands with Kenneth. "It was really nice doing business with you."

"Same here, but I guess this is all a huge joke. But since I doubt if I'll ever see you again, can you, at least, tell me your name?"

"I have quite a lot of names, but I think you can call me. Mr. Pestilence Although my full name would be Mephistopheles Pestilence but I guess that's too long a name for a man like yourself to remember. A good day to you, Kenneth." And with that, the man was no longer visible.

He had long disappeared, and Kenneth had seen him fade away. But he didn't quite believe — after all, there was a good possibility that he had hallucinated everything that he had just seen or done.

As he stumbled out of the bar into the cold air of the night, Kenneth knew he was going to have one hell of a hangover.

Chapter 6

Months rolled by in quick succession, and even though he went for his regular check-up with Doctor Pecker, there was still no cure to his cancer. The disease remained, but somehow, he didn't feel sick. He was, in fact, as strong as a wild horse.

"I don't get it. The cancer cells have not vanished, and nothing is happening to you. Technically, you're not cured, and you're not even dying – everything just seems normal." Doctor Pecker said in astonishment.

"I guess it's one of those mysteries in life that modern medicine will never solve, I'm just happy to live knowing that I'll see the next day. I just think of it as some sort of miracle," Kenneth replied.

"It sure is, Kenneth. Here was I, thinking that I would have to drop flowers on your grave before heading to the country club every afternoon," Doctor Pecker joked, and they both exploded with laughter.

After he came back home from the clinic, he sat at his rocking chair in the middle of the room, smoking his pipe. Mr. Pestilence had granted his wish, Mr. Pestilence, which he had considered to be unreal. But here he was, about eleven months later, still alive.

Kenneth suspected that the wish he had made was the mitigating factor as to why he had not been totally cured of the malignant disease. He had asked for immortality and not a cure. So, he was immortal and immune to the disease, which still remained uncured in his body. Kenneth was quite satisfied with that anyway – it was way better than dying.

"Hello, Kenneth." The voice came at him suddenly, and he almost fell off his rocking chair. It had come from behind his back. Turning around slowly, he was soon standing face to face with Mr. Pestilence.

"Mr. Pestilence …" Kenneth managed to croak, "How did you even get in? How can you be here?"

"Oh, no door is ever really locked to me. You look quite well, my friend. How's that cancer?"

"Well, I still have cancer. But I no longer feel any of the symptoms, and I have not died yet, as you can see. However, according to the town's doctor, the ailment still remains uncured." Kenneth replied.

"Yeah, I granted only what you asked me for - immortality. I hope you don't get bored too soon because it can be very boring – that's why I kill time by going around offering fair deals," Mr. Pestilence grinned.

"I suppose that you're here to collect your own part of the bargain. Seeing that you have kept yours," Kenneth noted.

"You're such a bright man, Long, of course, I'm here for the deal. But we won't be starting immediately. Just get prepared, we'll be starting soon, I only came to remind you," Mr. Pestilence said.

"I'm ever ready to serve you. I hope that our deal still stands even after my work for you is done?"

"I don't actually renegade on my deals, Kenneth. Trust me, I don't," and with that, Mr. Pestilence dissolved into smoke, and Kenneth went to bed.

***

No one knew how the Black Plague came to be, but it began exactly in the year 1967 in the little town of Chessington, Nebraska.

Bodies blackened beyond recognition, tongues swollen and dark like black tar, skulls visible, filling the once fresh air with the acrid smell of rot and decay.

But one man knew what was happening, and he didn't die in the Black Plague that wiped out Chessington. Instead, he lived on, moving from one city to another – and wherever he went, the Black Plague came.

SOMETHING'S WRONG WITH LEX

Chapter I

LEX WENT FOR THE BOWL OF CRUNCHY BONES. As far as he was concerned, life couldn't be better. Munching on his crunchy bones, which were really just buttered biscuits shaped like crossbones, he ruminated in his dog's mind about the family that had taken care of him since he was a pup.

He particularly liked the boy, the boy who always bathed him diligently every night before going to bed, who always played Toss the Frisbee with him, who always took him down for a walk when he was bored and longing for some excitement. But most importantly, Lex, who was also called Bessie, liked the boy because he always brought the bowl of Crunchy Bones.

The yard in which the house was located was quite beautiful. Lex's doghouse was just at the extreme of the wooden fence, beautified by the well-trimmed lawn, and a large oak tree that was surrounded by shrubs. It had been built specially for Lex through the combined effort of the boy and his younger sister.

A menacing and huge German Sheppard, Lex was quite a dog. With powerful hind legs, sharp eyes that could hardly miss anything even though he was growing quite old, ears that stood at alert and a ridiculously black nose that countered the brown color of his fur.

He barked excitedly as the boy approached, holding the pack of Crunchy Bones; Lex could tell that he was going to have another helping of the cereal. The boy who was Dennis Waller fell to his knees and refilled his dog's bowl.

"Hey boy, don't rush your food. Big doggie! Big, big, doggie!" Dennis cried excitedly as he embraced the dog. Lex squirmed under the boy's body and buried his face deep into the bowl.

Dennis Waller broke up the embrace and watched his dog. Even though he was only about ten years old, he could see that Lex had grown to be as tall as he was. The dog was just getting bigger and bigger by the day, and this was something that Dennis was proud of.

"Dennis, what are you doing out there this hot afternoon?" Mrs. Waller called; she had been busy spreading out the laundry at the back of the yard.

"Nothing, Mom, just feeding Lex. He seems so excited and hungry today," Dennis replied.

"Okay. Don't take too long; I need you back in so you can arrange your room —all those littered comic books and posters. You have to put them away." His mother paused and added. "Also, your sister needs help with her colouring, be a good boy, and help her."

"But Mom, I have to take Lex for his evening walk soon," Dennis protested. He hated having to put up with his seven-year-old sister, Sharon. She could be a real pain in the ass if she so wanted.

"No buts, Dennis. You can take Lex for a walk after you're done with helping your sister. Now, off you go," his mother said with a note of finality.

Dennis sighed heavily, got up from his crouched position beside the dog, and brushed off bits of sand from his denim jeans. Patting the dog on the head, he said. "Not to worry, Lex, you still get your evening walk as soon as I'm done with Sharon," he winked at Lex, who just looked on after him as the boy trotted away.

Lex didn't really understand what the boy had said, but it made him quite sad that he wasn't going to be having his evening walk anytime soon. He watched the boy go, soon the boy disappeared into the house and Lex went back to devouring bits of the cereal that remained in the bowl.

One thing about being a dog, which most animals didn't possess, except for wolves, coyotes, and foxes, which were still related to dogs, was the sense of alertness and self-consciousness. And it was this trait that now alerted Lex, as he looked up sharply.

His eyes were fixated on the old oak tree, the only one in the yard that was surrounded by tall shrubs. The shrubs seemed to be moving – like something was tangled in between them, giving off a rustling sound that made Lex growl under his breath.

This growl was only instinctive.

Over the years, since he had been with the Wallers, ever since they had moved to Shade Hills in Portland, he had always been encountering squirrels, woodchucks, and sometimes – quite rarely, owls.

On a certain occasion, he had been playing with his rubber ball with the boy and girl in the yard before they had left him alone to have their lunch. Lex had been alone in the yard when a certain woodchuck had shown up, apparently getting into the yard through a part of the fence that had been broken.

Lex, quite bored, had given it a hot chase. He pursued the woodchuck that scrambled away in panic from the menacing German Sheppard. The woodchuck would have been clamped in between his mouth if it had not somehow run down a hole at the back of the oak tree. Lex looked down this hole, it was a wide hole – no bigger than a bunched up fist, but it was large enough for the woodchuck to get in and for Lex to stick his nose through, sniffing for the scent of the woodchuck which he still wanted to have.

That was a grave mistake. Only that Lex didn't know this until he felt a sharp, searing pain on the muzzle of his nose. He howled and yapped loudly, moving away from the hole. His eyes watered as he howled in pain again. It was just sheer luck that the boy and his father had come out of the house just in time to see Lex sprawled on the floor.

He had been bitten by a night adder, probably one of the most venomous snakes in Portland. The man rushed at Lex and carried him off to the vet while the boy sniffled at the terrible sight of his dog. Well, in the end, he had been given an anti-venom that had countered the venom in his bloodstream.

Even though they never saw the snake, the man had taken his time to block the hole completely, filling it up with sand and plastering it over. They also repaired the wooden fence, and even though Lex was sorry that he would no longer get to pursue rodents or squirrels that often came through the hole, he was quite happy that he wouldn't have to be bitten by a snake again. It was a worse off experience that he never wanted again. That was about three years ago, and he had not seen any other animal since then.

He growled loudly now, approaching the shrubs that shook harder. The rustling sound had intensified, and Lex could bet that there was something in between those shrubs. He could even smell it. That smell was not very pleasant; it was an unfamiliar smell — like something soaked up in thick mucky mud.

As Lex probed the shrubs, he was careful not to allow his muzzle touch the grass, lest he got bitten again, but he was, at least, almost sure that whatever was in the shrubs was definitely not a snake.

And he was right.

For as he parted the shrubs with his forepaws, he was met with a pair of red eyes; eyes that glowed like red rubies in the dark.

Lex backed off and tried to bark but only a shrill 'woof... woof...' escaped through his mouth. He was utterly drained of terror.

Chapter 2

It was only a rabbit that Lex had seen in between the shrubs. But it didn't look like a normal rabbit. Certainly not like any rabbit that he had ever seen in his life as a dog.

The rabbit was staring right back at him. Its whiskers twitched, and its red eyes widened as if it were excited by the presence of Lex.

Lex, still somewhat terrified by the rabbit, finally let out a bark that ripped out of his mouth in a less hoarse way. But the dog was careful not to move closer to the rabbit – whatever that thing that was staring back at him was; it was no rabbit.

Back at the house, Dennis Waller, who was still helping his sister out with her coloring assignment, glanced anxiously at the window. He could hear Lex barking. Although, this wasn't something strange because Lex barked unnecessarily most times. However, there was something that bothered him about the bark – it was almost similar to the bark that he had heard when that snake had bitten Lex.

"What's wrong with Lex?" Sharon asked, googling at her brother, "Is someone in our yard?"

Dennis glanced at her; it was as if she was reading his thoughts. "Don't really know, Sharon, one way to find out though, let's check it out."

"Okay," his sister agreed; she was always ready for an adventure or two – and this time, Dennis was glad she was up for it. He was really starting to get worried about Lex.

"But don't mention it to Mom, we're supposed to be doing your coloring," Dennis said.

"I won't," she replied, pouting her lips. "Promise me that you'll allow me pet the doggie."

"Alright, but not too much, we have to be back up before Mom realizes that we're in the yard."

At this, Sharon only nodded her head.

Having gotten his sister to agree, they proceeded down the stairs of the house noiselessly. They could hear an ongoing TV commercial while the blender whirred loudly in the kitchen. Their mom was definitely too occupied to hear them go out.

Once in the yard, Dennis hurried towards Lex, who was still barking his head off at the strange rabbit in the shrubs. The dog glanced at them as they approached and directed its gaze back at the rabbit.

There was no rabbit anymore. All that was there were only the tall grasses that characterized it.

Falling on his knees, Dennis probed Lex's body, looking for any injuries. "Quiet boy, why getting so excited anyway?"

"Doggie, doggie…" Sharon sang rubbing Lex on the head, and he, in turn, licked her hand, which made her giggle.

Sometimes, he liked the girl too. Although he had a little trouble with her each time she tried to ride him like a horse.

Lex barked again at the shrubs, and this time Dennis was able to have a faint idea of what was getting the dog excited. He went over to the shrubs and searched through it, but there was nothing there anyway.

Turning to Lex, he said, "See, there's nothing here, old boy. Why were you barking so loudly at a bunch of grasses?"

Lex only sniffed the air in response.

And that was when Sharon tapped her brother on the shoulder. "Look, Dennis, what is that?" she asked, pointing at a black figure at the other side of the fence.

Chapter 3

Dennis glanced at the fence, but maybe a little too late. Whatever Sharon had seen was long gone. He frowned at his sister – thinking that she was probably up to her tricks again.

"Very funny, Sharon," he muttered.

"Not a trick, I actually saw something there. Yes! Mr. Rabbit," she declared as if she had just won a prize for knowing.

Dennis only furrowed his brow. "Let's get back inside before Mom notices that we're not upstairs. Stay right here, Lex, and no more barking. If you're a good boy, perhaps we can still get to walk later."

With that, Dennis and his sister headed back into the house, and Lex only allowed himself lie down on the lawn. As night approached – the boy never did come back for the walk as promised, but Lex found his way back into his doghouse. There would be more walks to come; he reminded himself before he drifted off to sleep.

Clouds in the sky exposed the moon, and lights back in the house flickered off. Somewhere in the shrubs, behind the old oak tree, the black rabbit watched and waited - its red eyes gleaming with anticipation.

Chapter 4

Something woke him up. It had ripped him out of his fluffy dog dreams and dragged him back to reality. Lex peered out of his doghouse. The night sky was filled with stars, and the moon was half-hidden by a passing cloud.

He yawned and stretched his body, going low a bit and extending his forearms. Then he scratched his ear with his hind leg; damned flies could be a menace sometimes.

The house was still dark, and Lex could guess that it wasn't going to be morning anytime soon, not that he was bound by time, but he really couldn't wait for the first light of day. His stomach rumbled he was also starting to get hungry.

His eyes darted towards the shrubs surrounding the oak tree. Something was there, watching him. Growling deeply, he trotted towards the shrubs, not moving too fast or slow – and was soon standing just in front of the tree.

The deep rumbling growl was still brewing at the back of his throat as he hunched over and approached the shrubs, picking his steps one by one.

When he had gotten close enough, the same pair of red eyes stared right back at him. Lex yelped and moved back.

The rabbit came out the shrubs, twitched its whiskers, and bolted away. Lex barked loudly after it and suddenly, gave it a hot chase. For a rabbit, this was sure faster than any creature that he had encountered. It darted forward and swerved away from Lex's line of attack.

Lex simply kept barking as he chased the rabbit, and just as he was about to lunge at it for one last time, the rabbit slipped through a large hole that had been created under the fence. Lex stood, sniffed the ground that led to the hole and dug furiously at it. Then he somehow managed to slip through the hole and went after the rabbit.

Chapter 5

Seeing the rabbit running away from him only excited Lex so he gave chase. Of course, he was no longer within the confines of the yard but was now following the rabbit down the road, which led to Shade Hills woods. So far, he could not make out where the rabbit was; but the smell which Lex had somehow registered was still strong, and this was what he followed.

He sniffed the ground, tracing the smell. It was pretty easy, maybe as easy as following a small trail of footprints in the sand. The smell of the rabbit gave him a sense of direction as to where it had followed, and he moved ahead, passing by low willow trees that waved thick branches in the dark, past the silent hooting of owls and twisted crawlers that seemed to have holes in the barks.

Lex turned around and sniffed the air, following the smell to one of the twisted crawlers – this particular one was at the extreme of the Shade Hills woods, which was overlooking the cemetery.

As he approached the crawler, bats perched on the tree, scattered into the midnight air. Lex barked at the tree and hunched over his shoulders, ready to strike whatever came from within the hole in the bark. The rabbit came out, stood on its hind legs, glaring at Lex.

It started to transform. Slowly, it transformed, shedding away the shape of the rabbit – that wasn't its true form. It became something hollow; it had long arms that looked like tree branches, with extended fingers that were sharper than normal. Its entire body was covered in dried autumn leaves that shook as it transformed.

Lex whimpered as it watched this strange creature, and finally, its red eyes popped up where its head should be. Lex barked at it bravely, moving back with each step as this creature approached.

Then it broke into a wild run, away from the evil that had emerged from the crawler tree, away from the creature that wasn't even a rabbit after all. But the dog hardly made it far. The tree thing that wasn't really a rabbit summoned vines that wrapped themselves around the poor dog. Lex struggled, biting at the vines that seemed to have emerged from the crawler tree. The vines bound his entire body and squeezed tightly, blocking off his flow of blood and his lungs. The dog whimpered again, struggling feebly and was soon still.

The tree thing, satisfied that it had completely maimed the dog, controlled the vines again, which unwrapped themselves from the body. It opened its wide mouth, which wasn't really a mouth and devoured the dog.

Slowly, it transformed again, taking up the features of the meal it had just had. It would be getting a much better meal soon.

Chapter 6

"Mom, have you seen Lex?" Dennis asked. He had been to the yard, quite early, holding the pack of Crunchy Bones alongside Lex's bowl. But the dog was nowhere to be found.

"He's probably at the back, honey," Mrs. Waller replied. The door swung open and Mr. Waller, who had worked in his study all night on a new article, was up and ready for work.

"Dad, I can't find Lex, got any idea where he could be?" Dennis asked.

His father's eyes grew wide with surprise, "What do you mean? Lex has never ever left his doghouse before. He's probably holed up inside there, at the far corner — snoozing away."

"He's not, Dad; I have checked the whole house," Dennis said sadly.

"Alright, let's find that old boy, there's no how he could have wandered out of the house, the gates were locked. I personally saw to that. Isn't that right, honey?"

Mrs. Waller nodded in agreement, "Yeah, there's no how Lex could have gotten out of the house."

"Not to worry, Dennis, let's just do a routine check; you'll see that Lex is probably just outside anyway or at the backyard," his father said. They both left the kitchen while his Mom fixed breakfast and hollered loudly to Sharon, who was still in bed.

Everything outside was bright, the sun sent down warm rays, which made the day worth looking forward to. Their first stop, in their search for Lex, was the doghouse.

Of course, it was empty. There was no sign of Lex there, anyway. Both father and son called at the top of their voices, but there was still no sign of Lex.

"I'm starting to get worried, Dad. What if something or someone carried Lex away?" Dennis asked. Tiny streaks of tears were forming at both corners of his eyes.

"Hey, hey, Champ. No need getting worked up. We'll find Lex. I promise you that – he's probably holed up somewhere in the house, maybe he even found a way into the house – ever considered that possibility?" his father soothed.

Dennis, who had almost lost hope, had felt a surge of excitement at the prospect that Lex could be down in the basement of their house; it was, at least, quite possible that he had somehow found his way in – through the kitchen or maybe the back door.

"Let's check it out. I'm pretty sure we'll find him there," his father declared. They headed back into the house and searched the basement and even went for the attic, but Lex was nowhere to be found.

"Dad, Dennis! Come and see!" Sharon shouted, her voice was coming in from the yard – it was almost 7:45 am and the school bus was sure to be around the corner soon.

Dennis bolted outside with his father right behind him. They soon saw what Sharon had cried about – just behind the old oak tree, there was a large hole dug under the fence.

"Dad…" Dennis said, almost dreamily.

"Yeah, I see it too, Champ. He probably dug his way out, and look," his father pointed at another hole that seemed to have been gnawed open by something with teeth. "It appears that he was chasing after something."

Denny crouched down and examined the hole. His father was definitely right; Lex must have been after something that really would have made him dig a hole large enough for him to wriggle out of the fence.

Tears filled his eyes, "Will he ever come back home?" this question was directed at no one in particular.

"Stop being a baby," Sharon teased.

"Shut up," Dennis snapped at her. "He's gone, Dad." He added almost quickly.

His father wrapped him up in an embrace. "Not to worry, Champ. Something tells me that Lex will find his way back home."

"But he has never been out of the house on his own before, do you think he'll be able to find us back on his own?" Dennis asked, still sobbing.

"I'm pretty sure that Lex is smart enough, he'll come back home, oh, there's the bus – don't wanna miss school now, do you?" his father announced. True enough, the bus was parked and waiting for them.

Sharon hurried off with her lunch box and school bag, while Dennis tottered after her. He couldn't simply bring himself to terms with the fact that Lex could be gone forever. His father slipped in an extra ten-dollar bill into his pocket and kissed him.

"Perhaps, you never can tell if Lex would be back home by the time you get back from school, so no need getting sad," his mother added, kissing him and wiping off his tears.

With these assurances, Dennis was able to find his way to school. Even though he tried very hard to concentrate on his math, reading, and baseball practice – his mind kept going back to Lex. Where could his dog be? What had exactly happened the night before?

But he was in for a surprise. Like his mother had predicted, Lex did come back home.

Chapter 7

The tree thing that wasn't Lex emerged out of the bark of the crawler. Usually, after feeding, there was a huge tendency of it getting quite weak before its transformation could be complete. It was the only way for it to survive.

For centuries, since its arrival from the Ether Dimension, it had thrived on animals – basically because this had been enough to sustain it. But after feeding – it had always relapsed into some kind of hibernation, a sleep cycle that lasted for about a year. The tree thing had stopped being satisfied with that, and then it had hit jackpot when it discovered the Wallers.

All it needed was something that would guarantee its continued existence, a means of going on without finally dying away. Shapeshifting was to its own advantage; it had always been able to replicate the features of any animal that it had killed – this was only a mechanism that allowed it to get more prey.

With its transformation finally complete, it trotted down the lane, which led out of the woods and crossed the road, which led back to the Wallers' house. It knew that the absence of the dog would have been obvious – but it also knew that no one would be suspicious if it showed up again in the form of the dog. It had to be careful, there were certain traits about the dog that it had mastered and studied – maybe not well enough due to the limited amount of time, but well enough to aid in its mission.

It was hungry for more flesh and was going to have it. The house was quite dark as it approached. Night had come faster than it had anticipated since its last meal. It came over to the fence and was quite surprised to find that the broken fence had not been mended yet. This was a good thing, it reasoned. They were still expecting the dog to come back.

It wriggled through the broken fence and made its way to the doghouse. It was still very hungry. There had to be something to eat – something to quench its thirst for blood. Blood was what drew it to the Wallers in the first place; the tree thing had a penchant for fresh blood.

It had watched day and night with increasing salivation, the boy and girl – they had fresh blood running through their veins, and their flesh was bound to be quite tender.

Lying down on the grass, the thing waited. By first light, it would announce its arrival with a bark – and yes, it knew the kids, most especially the boy, would be glad to have him back.

At this thought, the tree thing grinned wickedly and waited.

Chapter 8

Woof! Woof! came the loud barking of a dog, as early as 8:00 am. It was a Saturday morning, and Dennis was still in bed. Throughout the day before, after he had gotten back from school, he had sat by the old oak tree watching the fence anxiously.

Nothing was going to take him away from the fence until he was sure that Lex was back in the house. It had taken quite a lot of convincing to get him back into the house in time for dinner — which he didn't particularly enjoy anyway.

That same night, his dreams were filled with images of Lex. He tossed and turned on his bed restlessly, occasionally peering out of his window at the doghouse, hoping to catch a glimpse of his dog.

At dawn, he had gone back to bed and was slipping away when he heard the bark. Dennis shot out of bed like a rocket and hurried towards the window. Standing in the yard, yapping loudly at the direction of his window, was Lex.

"Lex!!!" Dennis cried excitedly and bolted out of his room; he flew down the stairs in such a hurry that he woke up his father, who swung open the door of his room frantically — fearing the worst.

"Dennis, what happened?" he asked.

"Dad! It's Lex! He's back outside!" the boy reeled out, "I just heard him bark now."

"Really?" his father said doubtfully and peered out the screen door, which allowed a direct view of the yard. True enough, there was Lex, standing in the yard, barking hysterically.

"You see him, don't you, Dad?" Dennis furthered.

"Yeah, I certainly do see him, but he looks horrible, where the hell has he been?" his father wondered, they opened the door and headed into the yard. The tree thing that wasn't Lex ran towards the boy and pounced on him, licking his face, and this made Dennis giggle.

"Stop it, boy, where have you been? You had me worried," Dennis said, caressing Lex.

His father only smiled down at him. In a way, it was such a relief that the dog had somehow found the way back to the house; he had almost started getting worried for Dennis. In fact, Mr. Waller was already considering getting another dog for Dennis; this he hoped would set the boy at ease – just in case the dog never came back.

But here was the dog, maybe a little dirty but certainly still alive and here.

Mrs. Waller came out of the house, her nightdress fluttering about her. "What was all that fracas about?" she inquired, "Why, is that not Lex? He came back home on his own?" she added, kneeling beside Dennis.

"Yeah, I can't believe he found his way back, Mom," Dennis affirmed, still stroking the dog's fur.

"Lucky you then, but get him washed up, he looks very dirty and stinks like a forgotten refuse bin," his mother instructed.

"Okay, Mom, I'll get right to it," Dennis agreed.

Sharon came down later to see the dog but drew back in disgust when she saw that Lex's eyes were quite similar to that of the rabbit that she had seen about some days ago in the yard.

"Why does he now have Mr. Rabbit's eyes?" she asked her brother, who was busy running water all over Lex's fur while his father scrubbed the body of the dog.

"What do you mean?" Dennis asked, looking at his sister.

"His eyes are red, like that of the rabbit that Lex was barking at the other day." Sharon replied.

"Very funny that I never saw that rabbit," Dennis grunted. "Quit fooling around and go play with your dolls."

"But I'm not lying; it's true," she insisted, making quite a lot of emphasis on each word.

"Sweetie, why don't you go help your mom in the kitchen and bake some cookies? We'll soon get old Lex cleaned up in no time and come in to have a bite," their father winked at her.

Sharon stuck out her tongue at Dennis and hurried back into the house; it was the only way their father knew he could stop the inevitable argument that was about to start between the two of them.

After Lex was washed and cleaned, Dennis brought a full pack of Crunchy Bones for the dog. He poured this into the bowl and put it forward. But Lex didn't move towards the bowl, the dog just stood back regarding Dennis.

"Boy, I know you are very hungry, come and have your favourite," Dennis said, but the dog only stood looking at him. There was something chilling about the way the dog seemed unresponsive —as if contemplating an idea.

"Well, there's your food. Perhaps, you don't want me to see how hungry you are." Dennis shrugged and headed back into the house – he would get the leash and walk Lex as soon as the dog was done with the meal.

The tree thing watched the boy go and smiled. It was an insult that it was being offered a cereal when it needed flesh, but there was no need allowing the boy gets suspicious – the sister had grown to be more observant than the boy himself.

The tree thing that wasn't Lex decided to eat the Crunchy Bones cereal. In the end, it didn't taste really bad, but it was nothing compared to fresh blood and flesh, which it intended to, have tonight.

It knew it had to strike fast – this was because it stood the risk of being fished out by the girl, and this was something it couldn't afford.

The boy was soon back. He was most certainly surprised to find the bowl empty and patted the tree thing on the head.

"Good boy," he said. "Now, let's go stretch our legs a bit," the boy added, producing a leash.

The tree thing allowed itself to be leashed by the boy, and as they walked down the main street of Shade Hills, it schemed and planned on how it was going to get its first taste of human flesh.

CLOWN TOWN

Chapter I

COLLIE BREWSTER KNEW THEY OUGHT TO HAVE PASSED THE INTERSTATE ROAD, WHICH LED PAST FORT DOTTING. It was after all the only road, which would help them get to Texas easily.

But Michel Valve and Percy Dormouse thought differently.

"C'mon, don't be a bore, Collie. It's just a detour. We can't take too much time," Michel insisted. They were presently almost approaching the turnpike, which would have led them straight to Mile 81. Just ahead, Collie could make out an old mounted signpost, which had two arrow-shaped pointers that read: MILE 81 – STRAIGHT AHEAD TO HOUSTON, TEXAS and FORT DOTTING – DOWN THE BEND TO CLOWNSVILLE.

Clownsville was definitely an awkward name for a county.

"Look, guys, I agreed to come on this road trip only because you promised me that we would stick to the rules," Collie declared almost exasperated.

"Yeah, yeah... Don't be a sissy man. Like Michel said, this is only a detour; we're just gonna grab a few packs of beer, refill the gas and be on our way. No need getting worked up." Percy chipped in.

Collie sighed and allowed himself plop back in his seat inside the Dodge Ram. The truck itself belonged to Percy's father, who had only allowed the boys take the truck on the promise that they would stick to the main road, avoid going over the speed limit, and not drink while driving.

But the moment the car hit the road, all those rules were pretty much out the window as soon as Michel turned on the ignition, and Percy was riding shotgun. Collie himself could do nothing once the other guys set their hearts to it.

"Relax, Momma's boy; I bet this is actually your first time going on a road trip all on your own – with us, as guides, of course." Michel chuckled, swerving past the mounted sign.

"Fuck you," Collie muttered.

"Oh, that has gotta hurt, hit a nerve, didn't I?" Michel teased. They both fell silent as the truck galloped on scattered stones that characterized the road, which led towards Fort Dotting. The dust being flared up obscured the view ahead, but Michel managed to drive the truck through.

Overhead, it was getting quite dark already. They were soon speeding past rows and rows of endless cornfields, barns and old houses that had banged up shingles. A little further, they went past an old church, which seemed like it had not seen a congregation in years and were soon down the road. There was a gas station there; a no-smoking neon sign flickered on and off as the Dodge Ram moved in and halted to a stop in front of one of the pumps.

"You and I know that we don't really need that much gas, considering that we only filled it up about two hours ago," Collie protested.

"True," Percy agreed. "But you don't wanna be stuck in a backcountry road now, do you? Trust me, the possibility of getting robbed or worse still murdered, are endless here."

"And you still allowed Michel take this route." Collie spat out angrily. "Damn, what the hell was I thinking when I agreed to follow you guys?"

"The Houston Chicks," Michel winked at Collie as they all approached the screen door, which had the sign on it flipped to: CLOSED.

"Oh, great, can we just get back into the car and continue our so-called road trip?" Collie whined, "Or do we still have to wait for the unknown gas station owner?"

"Right you are, Collie. We're going to look around for him, he couldn't have gone too far anyway, seeing that the main screen door is unlocked," Percy noted.

"Don't know about you, but I ain't leaving until I have stocked the back of that truck with, at least – two packs of Budweiser beers," Michel added.

Collie only shook his head. It was actually no use arguing with the boys. So, he simply tagged along with them as they snooped around the gas station store, he just hoped the local who had the store wouldn't point a gun at them for loitering around the gas station.

"Really, what's the fun in going on a road trip, if we don't make little detours like this? It would be totally boring, Collie. I know you're most anxious to get to that beach and see that little girlfriend of yours," Percy winked.

"Snap out of it, let's just get in the store and buy whatever we want, fill the gas and drop the money on the table – got a really unpleasant feeling that the gas station owner might not be too pleased with us snooping around," Collie suggested.

"Alright, that's a good idea," Michel agreed, and all three of them, with Collie in front, pushed open the screen door, which creaked open.

The store was fairly large; there were rows of plastic cans, which definitely contained break oils, lubricants, and different batteries for cars. At the right side was the clerk's counter. There was no one there now, and at the extreme of the store were provisions, drinks, and all sorts of liquor stacked up not too far away from the fridge.

"There's the fridge," Percy said, pointing at the fridge. "We should most likely get the beers right there."

"Yeah, c'mon Collie, let's go check it out," Michel announced, but Collie kept to his position, standing quite close to the clerk's counter.

"I had better stay, there's a possibility that whoever owns this place is not too far off – and I'll be able to explain things to him. Trust me; he won't be very happy that we actually came in without him being around." Collie replied.

"Okay, your loss." Michel headed towards the fridge while Collie only looked on, waiting for the gas station owner.

Percy, on the other hand, was thumbing through a pile of magazines that were just on the left side of the store. He waved a Playboy magazine towards Collie, "I bet your girlfriend's gonna be in the last edition."

Collie flipped him the bird.

However, before he could turn around, something as cold as steel was pressed at the back of his head.

"Any funny business, young man, and I'll spray your brains on my counter," came the thick voice of an old man.

Chapter II

"Whatcha doing in my store, boy?" the voice continued, "Came to grab some stuff, right?" Collie could almost tell that the man had a thick Southern accent.

"So sorry, sir, my friends and I are simply just on a road trip. We decided to get some gas, so we stopped over here, there was no one in the store, so we thought we could just take what we wanted and put the money on the counter," Collie explained. The nozzle of the gun was still pressed against the back of his head.

"Not very wise, boy; you should have waited. By the way, where are these friends?" the voice furthered.

Collie only replied by pointing ahead.

At that same moment, Michel appeared, holding two packs of beers stacked up on each other, his eyes grew wide with fear when he saw the old man and the gun pressed against Collie's head.

"Don't move boy, stay just where you are." The old man instructed, "Yeah, drop the beer and step over here."

Michel, who was still frozen with fear, had hardly moved before Percy bumped into him from behind, holding a bunch of Playboy magazines.

"What the heck—" Percy started to say before he also noticed the old man. The magazines slipped from his grip, and he raised his hands up in surrender.

"Look, sir, I'm not lying. We only just made a detour to Fort Dotting. Just to get the gas and some beers, we have money…" Collie stated, trying to put his right hand into his pocket.

The gas station owner only nudged him with the gun, "No need doing that son, I believe you." The man declared, putting down the gun and heading over to the counter. Collie turned around and finally caught a clear glimpse of him. He was a bit tall, with flowing white wavy hair that fell to his shoulders in graceful tresses. The old man was also dressed in a flannel shirt over a pair of jeans and boots.

"You do?" Collie asked in surprise.

"Sure, you guys don't look like no marauders, that's for sure. But next time, if you don't see a store owner, kindly wait. Most locals here are fucking trigger happy." The old man advised.

"Thanks, sir," Michel said, he was still standing over the packs of beer on the floor.

"That's fine, pick up your beer, and you can have the Playboy magazines, no one looks at them here anyway," he addressed Percy, who was looking to put back the magazines.

"Thanks, how much does the beer cost?" Collie asked, pulling out his wallet.

"About five dollars and seventeen cents," the old man replied. Collie handed the man about six dollars, and Michel, in turn, paid for the gas, which totaled around fifteen dollars.

"So, where are you boys headed?" the old man asked.

"Just Houston, we're on a road trip," Percy replied.

"Is that so?" the old man furthered, this time, directing the question at Collie.

"Yeah, it's a road trip, alright, we're on summer holidays. It was Michel's idea anyway – I'm not much of the outdoor type," Collie answered.

Michel grinned. "He's a Momma's boy, good sir." At that, both he and Percy exploded into a fit of laughter, and the old man joined them. Collie's face was quite flushed with embarrassment.

"Not to worry, Houston's a fine place. Been a while that I went down that way. But why are you passing through Fort Dotting? That's like way off the mark," the old man noted.

"Well, we just decided to take another route. Is there a route that leads from Fort Dotting to Houston?" Michel asked.

"Yeah, but like I said, it's way off. You'd have to pass through Clownsville, which is about a few miles from here. My advice would be, turn around and take the Mile 81 route – it's pretty straightforward and faster than passing through Clownsville." The old man said.

"That was my thought exactly, but they wouldn't listen to me," Collie declared triumphantly.

"We know that route well enough, sir. But what's the fun in embarking on a road trip and taking familiar routes? It would only turn out to be quite boring if you ask me." Percy chipped in.

"Very boring, indeed." Michel agreed.

"Can you please talk some sense into my friends? It's a shame I can't drive." Collie groaned.

"No fault of ours." Both Michel and Percy chorused.

"Look, boys, I hardly know you guys, but I have taken a liking to you. If you'll take my very candid advice, I'll prefer that you guys turn around and take the fast lane down Mile 81. It isn't safe out there, especially passing through Clownsville," the old man informed.

"What do you mean?" Collie's calm demeanour was suddenly replaced with some kind of panic.

"Well, Clownsville has a certain history to it. Now, it's just basically a deserted town that has no residents whatsoever, at least, that's what the state government declared. However, there have been rumours that people who pass through the town disappear and are never found again." The old man looked at the boys gravely.

"That's a joke, right?" Percy asked.

"No, son, it's no joke. Lots of travelers, drifters, and tourists who want to see the famous circus town always end up being reported missing – none of them are ever seen again. It's hard to believe, but rather true."

"How did this town, Clownsville, come to be?"

The old man simply pulled out a flask from his back pocket and drank from it. It was probably whiskey or gin, Collie thought.

"The town itself was established around the mid-eighties, it thrived mostly on tourists that came to watch its famous circus. Most of the town was filled with circus performers, gypsies, and clowns," the gas station owner replied, taking a swig from his flask. "About three years later, there was a fire that wiped out half of the town. With most of the residents dead, the traveling circus decided to pack up and leave; the town itself was declared closed." He concluded.

"That's a pretty good story, but how does that corroborate the fact that people who pass through the town or visit it disappear?" Michel chipped in.

"That has been quite a mystery if you ask me, but there has been little or nothing anyone could do about it. So, this is why I'm asking that you take the normal route to wherever it is you boys are going." The old man said, regarding each of the boys.

"Okay, we'll do just that. Won't we?" Percy grinned, patting Michel on the back. Collie, on the other hand, just kept silent.

"Thank you so much for your time, sir; I guess we'd be on our way," Percy said, shaking hands with the old man.

"Collie, c'mon, let's get going. It's almost dark." Michel called to Collie, who was still ruminating about what the old man had said.

He glanced at the old man and smiled, "So sorry; I guess I was still thinking about all you just said."

"That's fine. Just make sure you and your friends stick to the road – I know they might not take my advice, but you seem to be different from them. Even if you guys will go through Clownsville, don't even try to stop over there, just head on to the next town."

"Thanks," Collie said and headed out of the store.

The old man watched the boys go; somehow, he wished they'd follow his advice and head back down Mile 81. There was absolutely no need for anything to happen to them.

Chapter 3

"You heard what that old man said, let's just drive back to Mile 81 and get the rundown towards Houston." Collie said.

"Why should we do that? For all we know, that man could have just been trying to scare us for getting into his store without his permission," Percy replied.

"If you really believe that, then you're as dumb as I thought you were." Collie shook his head in indignation.

The Dodge Ram sped down the dusty road and was soon past another signpost that announced: WELCOME TO CLOWNSVILLE (LEAVE SOME OF YOUR FUN BEHIND). Only thing was, the signpost itself was almost broken — most of the words had faded, and it had taken Collie quite a few seconds to make it out.

"Not to worry, Collie, there's no one here. We'll not be stopping by anyway; we're just passing through, so quit whining and relax." Michel said; the faint light emanating from the dashboard cast a streak of light on his face.

Collie only fell silent once more at that.

Percy lighted a cigarette and puffed on it before exhaling sharply, blowing off smoke from his nostrils. "Pass me one of those beers, would you?"

"Sure, I could use one myself," Collie agreed and handed him the beer.

Nightfall made it almost difficult to see the road, so Michel turned on the headlights, which illuminated the road. Most of the town was obscured by the flared up dust, and they could hardly make out the buildings or houses that they approached.

The truck slowed down to a halt, and Michel turned off the ignition. Collie looked at him in utmost surprise. "Why did you stop?"

"Nothing, I'm kind of feeling a bit weary. I have been driving all day, why don't we just rest a little, then we can move out at first light?" Michel suggested.

Collie shook his head furiously. "C'mon man! Don't do this; you heard what that old man said about this fucking town, just get us outta here, then we can camp for the night."

"Stop yapping like a baby, Collie. I can assure you that nothing will happen to either of us, we can sleep it off at the back of the truck, but I was being very honest about being tired," Michel replied.

"Yeah right, you're just doing this intentionally," Collie muttered, he actually chided himself for not learning how to drive. If he could drive, he would have left them to their fate and headed out of Clownsville in a hurry. Something about the whole place gave him the creeps.

"Collie, give Michel a break. Just relax, we'll protect you from all the monsters in the closet." At this, both Michel and Percy exploded into loud fits of laughter.

Collie didn't smile. He didn't actually find it funny that they were in a strange town and trying to stopover. But there was little or nothing that could be done in the matter, and besides, Michel still held on to the keys.

They alighted from the truck and glanced around. Most of the buildings in the town were quite old, dilapidated and falling apart. There was the Municipal office, a motel, a barroom, and a small amusement park.

"HEY, LOOKIT!!" Percy screamed excitedly. "That's a mini amusement park, been long since I last saw one. I bet all the rides are still there too."

"Too bad you won't be getting into any," Collie chipped in.

"Well, that depends. I sure would like to try that roller-coaster again for one last time, who knows when I'd ever see one again." Percy said.

"Look, guys, why don't we just stay right where we are until dawn, and then you can get to ride in this roller coaster by morning."

"Nice idea," Michel agreed.

"I honestly don't know why you guys are just so scared of this town anyway; I haven't seen anything weird so far

— so much for the scary ghost story," Percy said, shaking his head.

Michel and Collie headed to the back of the truck while Percy stood at the other side of the road, answering the call of nature. It was such a relief; his bladder was almost as if it was on fire.

With his eyes closed, he didn't see the painted face of the clown, with tufts of orange hair at either side of the head watching him from behind the Municipal building. This clown had a red rubber nose and red lips that were drawn wide like a smiling emoji. Large pompom buttons graced the sleeved costume, and the clown was also wearing a pair of flip-flops.

As soon as Percy opened his eyes, the clown withdrew his head sharply. But Percy's peripheral vision had caught a tiny glimpse of a receding shadow.

He whirled around and faced the Municipal building. "What the fuck —" he managed to gasp out loudly.

This caught the attention of Collie, who hurried towards him. "Is there a problem?"

Percy didn't reply but hurried towards the building with Collie right behind him. "Hey, wait up. What's wrong, man? Did you see anyone?"

"I'm pretty sure you guys are just trying to scare me, for all I know, that could have been either you or Michel. Too bad for you, I'm way ahead," Percy said.

"What happened? Heard you scream, did your winkle get a stopper?" Michel joked.

"Shut up, Michel." Percy said, "I know you guys are trying to get me off guard. But I'm way sharper, wasn't that just you behind that building?"

"What are you talking about?" Michel asked in astonishment.

"You're telling me that you weren't just spying on me as I was taking a piss over there just now?" Percy asked.

"Nope, why would I do that? Ain't no creep."

"How about you, Collie?" Percy furthered.

"Percy, we were standing behind the truck all the while, we haven't moved around yet," Collie replied.

A cold chill ran down Percy's spine. "Then who was watching me? I can swear I almost caught someone spying on me from behind that Municipal building."

Chapter 4

"Spying on you?" Collie asked, "That's totally creepy. Can you guys now see why I was insistent on you not stopping here for the night?"

"Don't tell me you're still remembering what that senile gas station owner told you; as far as I'm concerned, there's no one here," Michel said, moving back towards the truck.

"Well, maybe it was only a figment of my own imagination." Percy shrugged, "Hell, I could use a beer, want one?"

Collie only shook his head. They were simply just determined to spend that night in Clownsville, and nothing was going to change their minds. Everything about the town creeped him out. He looked around nervously, hoping to see someone, but there was no one out there.

Michel and Percy slept at the back of the truck after chugging down about two bottles of Budweiser, while Collie settled down to sleep inside the truck.

Sleep soon eluded them, and once more, the night was silent in Clownsville.

Maybe not totally silent.

Several pairs of flip-flops whooshed and dragged along the gravel ground in the darkness. One of the clowns, simply known as Martinet the Bubbler, was twisting a rubber balloon. He twisted the balloon this way and that until it took the form of a rubber duck.

Another clown snatched away the balloon and popped it with a pin. Then this clown gestured towards Martinet to be quiet.

Martinet, having been scolded, crouched back on the floor and watched with the other clowns that numbered about six. They all looked hideous in their costumes, which comprised of flip-flops, rubber noses, and a tattered sleeved shirt with large pompom buttons. One of the clowns held a balloon by a string and grinned wickedly.

***

Percy's eyes snapped open. He had been having a bad dream – one that he couldn't quite remember too clearly. Someone had been after him, someone that held high a hatchet, dressed in a clown's costume and laughing hysterically.

That much was what he could actually remember before he managed to return back to reality. His shirt was soaked with sweat, and there was Michel beside him, snoozing away so easily.

The urge to pass urine came once more, and he jumped down the back of the truck, walked a little further towards where he had done it the day before, and proceeded to urinate. A soft chuckle floated towards him, and he turned around sharply.

Of course, no one was there. It was only the soft bellows of the midnight air that tousled his hair; it was only the soft thumping of loose shingles banging against the roofs of the deserted houses. Something passed beside him quickly, and Percy turned to face it again, but there was still nothing.

His heart raced faster than a formula one sports car in his chest, and he turned around with the bid of starting back towards the truck, he was standing face to face with a clown.

As a kid, Percy had always watched one particular show on TBS titled: BOZO'S HUB. This particular show was always about some dumb clown called Bozo, the Hobo, who performed stupid tricks like cycling with no hands, juggling and creating stuffs with balloons. The clown that Percy was looking at now was definitely a direct lookalike of that clown on TV.

But this thought was cut off as quickly as it was being formed. Something glinted in the moonlight and flashed across his neck. As Percy opened his mouth to talk, only blood spurted out in large streamlets. His hands shot up and wrapped around his neck to stop the heavy bleeding coming from his slit throat.

Slowly, his legs gave way, and he sank to the floor. A puddle of blood formed quickly, soaking up the gravel floor. The last thing he could see before his consciousness disappeared forever was the wide smile of the clown that looked like an emoji.

Chapter 5

Normally, he was in the habit of rolling over every other time he was asleep. He rolled over this time with hoping of hitting and annoying Percy, but his back only slammed against the other side of the truck.

"Goddamit, Percy, you can't even allow me to use you as my pillow," Michel said sleepily, extending his hand towards his friend; all he grabbed was thin air.

Rubbing his eyes, he stared around. "Percy?" No one replied.

Where the heck did he go? Michel thought. Pulling himself up, he jumped down the truck and looked around hazily. There was absolutely no sign of Percy. Was there even the faintest possibility that Percy had eventually gone to the mini amusement park? It was quite possible; Percy was full of rather crazy ideas.

Michel walked briskly towards the park. It was at the extreme end of the town. As he approached, he could make out cages that had been used to trap circus animals, wooden horses that served for the merry-go-round, a roller coaster, and candy shops, which were characterized by colored umbrellas and floating balloons.

At the very entrance of the park was a huge signpost with the words: WELCOME TO CLOWNSVILLE PARK, this particular signpost had the head of a clown on it — which was wide open in a frozen cackle.

Michel tore his gaze away from it and walked ahead, deep into the park.

He wanted to call out to Percy, but somehow, he didn't think it was such a good idea for one to be shouting at such a time in the night. It was already way past 1:00 am, and the only light that illuminated his path was the flashlight of his cell-phone.

Deep inside the park, he was soon closer to the gift shops when he noticed something rather odd. Someone was in the park with him; he squinted his eyes and drew closer.

There was a silhouette up ahead, Michel couldn't exactly tell from the distance. But it seemed the person was wearing flip flops and some sort of clown costume.

"Percy, is that you?" Michel called. But no reply came. He hurried towards the figure in the dark, trying very hard to make out who it was — the silhouette appeared to be juggling or doing an activity quite similar to juggling.

"Percy? C'mon man, this ain't funny. There you are, I bet you certainly don't want us to leave you behind now, do you?"

He stopped short when he realized that whoever he was talking to wasn't exactly Percy. It was a clown, juggling red balls and doing it with so much precision and accuracy.

One of the balls flew into mid-air, dropped on the ground, and rolled down towards Michel, who glanced down at it. His knees were knocking together. The clown turned around slowly and regarded Michel, who was by now, paralyzed with fear.

Michel could smell the rot and decay as it approached him slowly, the sleeved costume was charred up, and the head was as bald as a vulture's. But most revolting was the clown's face. There was actually no face, only huge plastic eyes that dripped with slime.

A scream must have escaped his throat; that was something he couldn't remember as he whirled around and ran. Never had he ever had to run as he had done at that very moment, but as he lunged ahead towards the entrance, he stepped on a rubber duck that made him slip, slamming his face, headfirst to the ground.

His nose shattered instantly, and blood poured out like a red river filling up his palm. Groaning loudly, he tried to stagger to his feet and was soon staring at dark figures that closed in on him.

Each clown looked similar, with their flip flops that made slippery sounds on the gravel ground as they approached him. They all had sharp knives that sparkled in the night. Michel screamed at the top of his voice as the stabbing ensued. But the scream didn't last very long as his lungs choked up with blood, and the darkness descended.

Chapter 6

Collie wouldn't have woken up if he had not heard the scream. At first, he thought it was probably just an unfinished dream that he managed to drag back to reality. But when the scream had intensified, he sat up almost immediately.

He pulled the door of the truck open and checked the back of the truck. There was no sign of Michel and Percy.

"Percy? Michel?" he said, almost tentatively. "Where the hell did they go?" the question didn't seem right to him. First, he scanned the Municipal building, followed by some of the houses, but of course, there was no one to be found.

Collie's eyes darted towards the mini-park and headed towards it frantically. Those fools, they were probably trying to play a silly prank on him. Well, he wasn't falling for it. He was soon in the park and searching for them.

He was barely past the roller coaster when he heard the humming sound. It was a steady low guttural sound that pervaded his auditory sense. Turning around, he was confronted with the most terrifying sight of his life.

Gathered around in a circle were several clowns, each dressed in costumes, holding rubber ducks, and moving around in flip flops that whooshed ceaselessly. But that wasn't what actually terrified him the most.

In the middle of the circle, dressed up as clowns, were the bodies of Michel and Percy. They had been propped up like dolls, with their faces painted and their noses replaced with rubber. Huge pompom buttons graced their sleeved overalls, and their lips were painted red.

Collie didn't scream. He muffled his own mouth with his hand and turned around racing for the truck. As he glanced behind his shoulder, one of the clowns had pointed at him, and the rest broke the circle, coming after him.

He broke into a run and headed towards the truck. Even though he lacked the knowledge of driving, the only option to survival and escape from the life-threatening situation that has already taken his friends' and is just some inches away from his own life too is the truck. He decided to trust his intuition and just drive. The door had been left unlocked, and the key was lying right on the driver's seat where Michel had eventually, unconsciously dropped it earlier before moving to the back of the truck to catch some sleep for the night.

Collie turned the ignition, as one of the clowns banged against the windshield with both fists. He put the truck into first gear and pulled the reverse backward as more clowns rushed at him.

Slamming his leg down on the accelerator, he lunged at them. The truck knocked one of the clowns away and plunged straight into the night as three more clowns came after him, but couldn't keep up with the gathering speed of the truck.

"I beat you, suckers!" Collie cried as he drove the truck at top speed, never releasing his feet off the accelerator. He couldn't steer the vehicle well, but he managed to find his way out of the Clownsville. That was all the young man could remember, as he woke up later in the morning to find himself lying on a hospital bed in Mile 81. He had had a crash after escaping Clownsville as a result of his inability to control the truck at the top speed he had driven.

The old man and his wife, who had rescued him from the scene, explained to him how they had found him unconscious, but still alive at the outskirt of Mile 81 and rushed him down to the hospital. Streaks of dried tears caked the face of the disheveled young man as he remembered his friends and the whole horror encountered therein at Clownsville.

THE AMNESIA SYNDROME

Chapter I

From: kylegates81@blueumbrella.com

To: darthvader29@blueumbrella.com

Subject: New Site!!

Message:

Dude, what the hell happened to your frigging phone? Been trying to contact you since you headed back to Arizona. How was your trip? Hope you did quite well with the whole website thingy? That aside, I was perusing the internet last night. Nothing really serious – Sundays back here in the Canyon are like being stuck in never-ending prayer sessions in a Pentecostal vortex. So boooring…

Well, that's not the crux of the issue; I was pretty much stuck at home. Mom had gone out to get some groceries in town. Did I mention that our ranch is like three miles away from the main town? Crazy, right? You have no idea. I can't even sneak out to the arcade anymore. Dad, on the other hand, had to fly back to New York. He finally got that contract he had turned in the proposal for. So, here I was, alone and bored.

I tried reading a few books at first (Dad just stocked up the library), but that didn't exactly work out – and mind you, my XBOX has been having issues since the last time we played it back in Bethesda. Dad tried fixing it for me, but it didn't quite work anyway. Now, I guess you can see how lonesome, hopeless, and bored I was.

Only good thing about this ranch is the Wi-Fi, a very good, strong signal that allows me to download lots of stuffs. Needless to say, I hacked the password, and boy, I can't even say how much files I have downloaded in the last few days. I went online, as usual, to get another game, having completed JUNGLE BALLS (by the way, I bypassed your record, check the online stats) when I saw this website.

I know you're probably curious about why I would be mailing you about a new website, but this is way beyond any porn site that I have seen. Forget about Kandy kisses, Silent ladies, or even King stars. This is the real deal, Darcy. Check it out and send me your thoughts.

The address is: http://torturelives.com

Expecting your mail back.

Your nerdy cousin,

Kyle Gates.

P.S: Don't you ever leave your browser history without clearing. Mom almost figured out what I was seeing over the internet.

P.P.S: SITE'S TOTALLY HARDCORE!

From: darthvader29@blueumbrella.com

To: kylegates81@blueumbrella.com

Subject: RE: New Site!!

Message:

Damn! How did you even stumble upon that website? I actually thought you were just huffing like you always do, you damned son of a gun. Well, I actually waited until it was way past midnight before I accessed it.

Neil's back home from college, and that dude just decided to become a thorn in my flesh. My room's not mine anymore, my gadgets, and even my closet. He's taking over the whole house, and my parents are really not doing anything about it. Tried complaining to Mom, but all she had to say was, "C'mon Darcy, be nice. He's your father's younger brother and your uncle." Uncle my foot! I've seen that guy shooting up dope. Dude's a bad influence on me. Anyway, I'm trying to stay on my grind. Can't afford him seeing the dirty stuffs I do every night.

Back to the case, in fact, I actually signed up on the website. You were totally right – no other porn site comes close. I even had to make sure there was some extra lube at hand. All those chains, ropes, nipple clamps, dildos, and vibrators – that's too much excitement for me to bear. I had to just do what needed to be done.

Noticed that there's paid membership on the site, too, for exclusive videos. I bet you didn't know that. I hacked old Neil's credit card information and mail. I'll probably be using that to sign up for those EXCLUSIVE videos (^_^).

I don't know what I'm going to get, but I know it'll be more intense than what I got in the free mode (which really did spike up my dopamine levels).

More updates as to how that turns out.

Thy Buster Buddy,

Darcy Wilshere.

P.S: Since the arcade is far from the ranch, why don't you bring the arcade home? Just saying.

Chapter 2

From: kylegates81@blueumbrella.com

To: darthvader29@blueumbrella.com

Subject: TAN?

Message:

Hey! Did you hear about TAN? Someone posted something on Twitter as regards it that correlates with Torture Lives (TL). According to the poster – they are offering live streaming for less than 12 bucks per hour. Pretty cheap? TAN starts off tomorrow, and I have gotten myself another lube. I bet old Mr. Kyle Dick can't wait for the next round. I'm hoping that I'll be able to watch the first live feed. Will you be online?

Kyle Gates.

From: darthvader29@blueumbrella.com

To: kylegates81@blueumbrella.com

Subject: RE: TAN?

Message:

Yeah, apparently, TAN means (Torture All Night), and I can't wait. I have gotten my exclusive membership, which sort of entitles me to certain special videos. Yup, I'll be online. I can't even give up anything for that.

Catch you online for the big event.

P.S: I'll be sticking to your clear browser history instruction henceforth; I was almost caught by Neil. I don't really know why he won't stop going through my stuffs.

From: kylegates81@blueumbrella.com

To: darthvader29@blueumbrella.com

Subject: Email from TL?

Message:

I was wondering if you got any email. Last night, I was actually on TL seeing one of the live feeds, yeah – the one that garnered up so much views. DOMMASTER'S CAGE was the name or something. Well, an email came through, and there were quite a number of attachments to it.

I haven't checked out the attachments yet, but the address was from: noreply@torturelives.com. I don't think I remember subscribing to newsletters or feeds – I don't have the privilege of getting a credit card like you.

So, is there even the wildest possibility that they sent a general mail?

Would check the contents of attachments later, going fishing with Dad.

Reply ASAP.

Kyle Gates.

From: darthvader29@blueumbrella.com

To: kylegates81@blueumbrella.com

Subject: RE: Email from TL?

Message:

I don't think I received any email with any attachments. Did you ensure that you actually checked the address? I mean, it could have been a spam mail – that happens a lot. DOMMASTER'S CAGE? It was totally crazy; I found myself actually wishing I was the one holding the whip and administering some really great lashes on Annie's behind.

I didn't mention in my last mail that I actually saw her with that bloke from Stokes High - some dude that wears a baseball jacket and a Red Sox cap. I just wish I could find a way to blast them off this planet.

Don't mind me for sounding so bitter; I'm just getting sick and tired of being turned down by every girl in my school. It really sucks to be me, honestly.

Can't believe I'm feeling quite depressed already; I had better go straight to TL. Catch you later.

Darcy Wilshere.

P.S: Don't fall into the river, and don't catch a disco trout.

From: kylegates81@blueumbrella.com

To: darthvader29@blueumbrella.com

Subject: URGENT!

Message:

Darcy, I know this might sound a little crazy, but please don't dismiss it as some kind of prank on my part. This is not a joke, and I'm starting to get really scared. Due to the fishing trip that I embarked on with Dad, I didn't have the opportunity of checking my mail until sometime around 7:20 this morning. As soon as I turned on my computer, lots of notifications streamed in; there was nothing unusual about this activity.

But I got a few feed links from TL and also an email about new videos, which I couldn't watch right away because I had another email. It was that same email address that I told you about, Darcy. The very same email address that had sent me the attachments that I have not gone through, and this time, there was a message that simply said, "Check this".

Now, here's where things get so weird that I feel like I'm starting to lose my mind. I opened the previous attachments, and I was shocked beyond my imagination. My hands are literally shaking typing this right now.

In each of the first five attachments that I received, there was a picture enclosed. Funny thing is; none of these pictures were in .jpeg format. It had actually been sent to me as pdf files, so I had to download directly – instead of having to view.

In the first picture, there was a guy – I can swear that he's not much older than me, he has his back turned towards the camera and he's bound to a bedspread eagle. There's some kind of bit-gag over his mouth and a leather mask covering his face, so I can't tell the color of his hair. These shots were taken at different angles, but there was no way of identifying his face. I sort of zoomed the picture and discovered bruises on the back of the guy in the pictures. But that's not what scares me, man.

I had woken up this morning to find my back covered in bruises – at first, I had simply dismissed it as minor injuries that I might have unknowingly sustained when I had gone fishing with Dad. Well, I don't really remember falling or hurting myself because if I did, I would remember, right?

But after seeing those pictures, I was forced to examine the bruises on my back again, and they sort of match what

I saw in the pictures of the guy that was sent to me. I hope I'm not sounding paranoid, but it's just the truth.

EMAIL ME BACK AS SOON AS POSSIBLE.

Kyle Gates.

CHAPTER III

From: kylegates81@blueumbrella.com

To: darthvader29@blueumbrella.com

Subject: YOU DIDN'T REPLY MY MAIL!

Message:

Why didn't you reply to my mail? Goddamit, Darcy, this is not a joke. I only just received another email from that same address. There are more pictures, Darcy, much more violent pictures, and each time I check these pictures, I find injuries on my body that I can't remember sustaining at the exact spots on the body of whoever is being sent to me.

Only yesterday, I was sent one picture, and this time, this guy is hanged from the neck, and a thin rope is used to bind his cock. Note that before I had checked my mail, I woke up this morning with a sore neck and a raging pain in my crotch.

Yes, I double-checked the picture; it was the same bruise with that of the tortured guy. I don't really understand; I don't fucking remember anything — Mom's starting to get suspicious because she thinks that I might be suicidal.

I heard her discussing with Dad in low tones this morning, and they have been acting weird around me lately - all this because I couldn't explain how I managed to get a swollen neck.

Darcy, please talk to me. You're the only person that can understand what's happening. Even though I have not seen the face of whoever is in the picture, I strongly believe that I might be the one. I do not know why this is, but that's the feeling in my gut, and I don't like it at all. I don't like it one bit.

Here's what is gonna happen. I'll send a message to whoever is sending me these pictures – I need to get to the bottom of this.

Your cousin,

Kyle Gates.

P.S: I have attached the pictures below, delete after viewing.

From:noreply@torturelives.com

To: kylegates81@blueumbrella.com

Subject: PRIVACY ISSUES

Message:

Hello, Mr. Kyle Gates.

It has come to our attention that you have been rather confused as to the identity of the individual in the exclusive photos that have been sent for your enjoyment. Do not worry about how we have gotten this information. We always ensure that our clients are monitored by the system so as to better serve you.

This shouldn't be a surprise to you seeing that you personally signed up for this. However, this leaves us to wonder why you have been sending these photos to a third party, who happens to be a member of our prestigious website. This is not a problem, but the service that is being offered to you is meant for inner circle premium members – your cousin does not, however, belong to this circle.

To avoid such impromptu emails from us in future, kindly ensure that your exclusive photos are kept and consumed for your own use alone. Further violations of this rule will only lead to termination of your membership and rather grave consequences, which we wouldn't like to go into detail on.

Mr. Kyle, we honestly hope that you'll follow this instruction it is in your best interest.

We'll be in touch; any further questions should be directed here.

The TL Team.

From: kylegates81@blueumbrella.com

To: noreply@torturelives.com

Subject: RE: PRIVACY ISSUES

Message:

You guys have gotta be kidding me! I never signed up for any exclusive membership. I don't even have a credit card that would enable me carry out such an online payment. This has got to be some kind of mistake. I can't remember doing all these things that you have directed at me.

I agree that I signed up on Torture Lives, but I did this registration only as a member that gives me access to free videos in the member forum. I never at any time upgraded to a paid membership, much less asking for exclusive photos and videos. Please, kindly review my profile, and you'll see that I'm telling the truth.

From:noreply@torturelives.com

To: kylegates81@blueumbrella.com

Subject: PAID MEMBERSHIP

Message:

Hello, Mr. Kyle Gates.

102

We verily assure you that there has been no mistake on our part. You not only signed up for paid membership but also our TAN program, which was launched about some weeks ago. Of course, this was strictly voluntary; we at Torture Lives can coerce no one to join our programme.

However, joining binds you automatically to our terms of service, which we take very SERIOUSLY. This shouldn't be much of a surprise to you. In other to better clarify things, here are some exclusive photos which were taken during last night's TAN session with you. We hope that this puts you in a better light of the situation.

We have also taken the liberty of attaching your paid membership form and credit card information in pdf format, for further clarifications.

Thanks for your patronage,

The TL Team.

From: darthvader29@blueumbrella.com

To: kylegates81@blueumbrella.com

Subject: STOP SENDING ME THESE PHOTOS.

Message:

What's up, buddy? I received your last two emails, but I deliberately did not reply you for some reasons.

I think you're right about everything, Kyle. But I want you to understand that I have no right to view such photos. I also received an email from the same address that has been sending you the pictures, and I was duly warned not to further discuss this issue with you anymore because you're an inner circle premium member. All our conversations are being monitored – that's something that I don't even understand.

I scanned my system for malware and all sort of viruses, but I still don't get how we are being monitored. Please, Kyle, I don't know what you did, but these guys are threatening me seriously.

I'm sorry, but I might have to temporarily block your email address – they said they would come after me.

So sorry,

Darcy Wilshere.

From: kylegates81@blueumbrella.com

To: darthvader29@blueumbrella.com

Subject: RE: STOP SENDING ME THESE PHOTOS

Message:

Darcy, don't you fucking do this to me. I woke up this morning with multiple injuries! I never signed up for any paid membership! You have to believe me, please. Some people are just after me; I see pictures of myself in different torture positions. The latest one was in some kind of gas chamber; I don't remember any of these things!

Help me, Darcy; I don't know who else to talk to.

Kyle Gates.

From:noreply@torturelives.com

To: kylegates81@blueumbrella.com

Subject: MORE PICTURES

Message:

Hello, Mr. Kyle Gates.

We want to thank you for complying with our last instruction. As you may well know now, we haven't been playing any kind of prank on you. You signed up for the membership out of your own free will, Mr. Gates. Nobody forced your hand.

It is, however, a wonder that you claim not to remember all these things and yet show up almost every night for your TAN sessions. We consider that to be quite ironic. However, we praise the swift action of your cousin who was expedient in taking himself off the matter. Like we postulated, this issue applies only to you and no one else outside the inner circle.

We look forward to tonight's TAN session – and we hope that you'll satisfy our viewers from all over the world and also promote the torture culture on which our website is built upon.

Any attempt to contact anyone else or tell your parents will only be counterproductive. We have taken measures to ensure close monitoring and surveillance. You can't contact the authorities on this issue because you fully signed up for this on your own – and of course, you're not a minor. We have taken the liberty of checking all records that connect to you in any way.

Our candid advice is to ensure that all remains under strict observance of our terms of service.

Finally, as a paid member and a regular volunteer for our TAN sessions, we have credited your local bank account with the sum of six thousand dollars, being earnings for work done for three weeks. We hope that this money will also gear you up into volunteering for more TAN sessions.

That's what Torture Lives is about. The pleasures are always endless, aren't you a living testimony to that fact, Mr. Gates?

We look forward to seeing you tonight.

The TL Team.

Chapter 6

From: kylegates81@blueumbrella.com

To: darthvader29@blueumbrella.com

Subject: (NONE)

Message:

I know you can't see my emails, but I don't have anyone else to turn to. This issue is driving me crazy. Morning after morning, night after night, new pictures that I have no memory of surfaces.

They keep insisting that I signed up for it. Darcy, you gotta believe me, I don't remember signing up for TAN or any paid membership on Torture Lives. I honestly regret signing up as a member on that website in the first place. I have sent you texts, voicemails and you just refuse to reply me.

Would it be worth mentioning that I haven't left my room in days now? Most of my body is covered in bruises and wounds that I can't explain. It's like I have holes in my memory that I can't seem to remember.

Help me, Darcy, please – just help me.

Kyle.

From: <u>kylegates81@blueumbrella.com</u>

To: <u>darthvader29@blueumbrella.com</u>

Subject: (NONE)

Message:

Damn you, Darcy. I'm in a lot of pain. Please help me.

If you'll not help me, I guess I'll take the easy way out. I have gotten some pills. Dad took me to see a psychologist. But of course, I couldn't have opened up on our dirty little hobby on the internet. I've been given several bottles of XANEX, which the doctor said will help me sleep and counter my depression.

I still get the pictures every night, and each picture comes out more degrading. I can't take it anymore.

I have written a letter to my parents – but I have left your name out of it. I know that you're only trying to save yourself from THEM. I wouldn't blame you. If you ever do read this email, know that I'll be dead. I have swallowed all the pills.

Never use Torture Lives again. It might be your turn next. You never can tell.

Goodbye,

Kyle.

STAY IN TOUCH

Thank you for reading my books, stay in touch for updates, and new book releases. Visit my website www.deardaughterslovesmom.com for more information. Please feel free to stalk me on social media, I am on; Facebook, Twitter, LinkedIn, and Instagram

More books by author Cheryl T.Long

1. Jaden (a sickle cell story) picture book (E book and print) now available
2. Pricilla Goes to Camp(A Cerebral Palsy story) E book) coming soon
3. The Adventures Of Robyn and Calico (E book and print) now available
4. The adventures of Robyn and Calico (The case of missing Soda Pop) picture book (E book and print) 10/2019
5. The adventures of Robyn and Calico (The case of missing Eggs) picture book (E book and print now available
6. Born in Between picture book (E book and print) now available
7. As the Flowers Bloom book 1(Cherish series) (E book and print) now available
8. Bursting of the Flower book 2(Cherish series) (E book and print) now available
9. Full Blossom book 3(Cherish series) (E book and print) now available

10. Sleepless Nights Murder Mystery (E book and Print) now available
11. Facing the Fear of being Alone (E book) now available
12. Love Yourself (E book) now available
13. How to deal with the silent treatment (E book)now available
14. How To Forgive When Your Heart Is Broken (E book) (release date 10/2019)
15. Dealing with Toxic People (E book)
16. Setting Healthy Boundaries   (E book) release date 10/2019
17. Exchanging Emotional Pain for Peace and Prosperity now available
18. Hayden (coming soon)
19. Letting Go And Letting God (E book) now available
20. Double Mindedness (E book) (coming soon)
21. The Benefits of Learning Self-Worth (E book) (coming soon)
22. How to meditate (E book) (coming soon)

Follow me